My Adventure with HAROLD and the PURPLE CRAYON

Activity Book

T0063677

HarperFestival is an imprint of HarperCollins Publishers.
My Adventure with Harold and the Purple Crayon Activity Book
Copyright © 2022 by The Ruth Krauss Foundation, Inc.
All rights reserved. Manufactured in Italy. For information address HarperCollins
Children's Books, a division of HarperCollins Publishers, 195 Broadway, New York, NY 10007.
www.harpercollinschildrens.com
ISBN 978-0-06-265528-8
22 23 24 25 26   RTLO   10 9 8 7 6 5 4 3 2 1
❖
First Edition

My Adventure with
HAROLD
and the
PURPLE
CRAYON
Activity Book

Based on the character created by
Crockett Johnson

HARPER FESTIVAL
An Imprint of HarperCollinsPublishers

You're about to embark on an epic adventure with Harold!

Whenever you see this

---

draw over the dashed lines with your crayon.

Let's practice!

Whenever you see this

place your crayon on the dot labeled 1. Draw a line to the dot labeled 2. Then to the dot labeled 3 and so on in numerical order until all the dots are connected and you reveal the picture!

Let's practice!

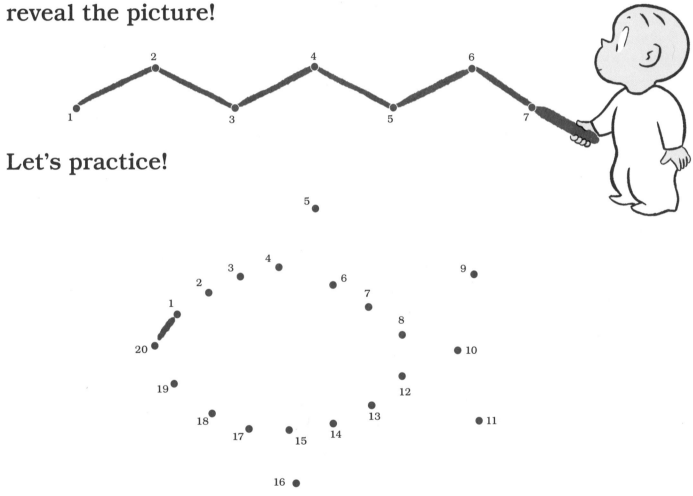

Look out for other activities throughout your adventure! An answer key is at the back of the book. Have fun!

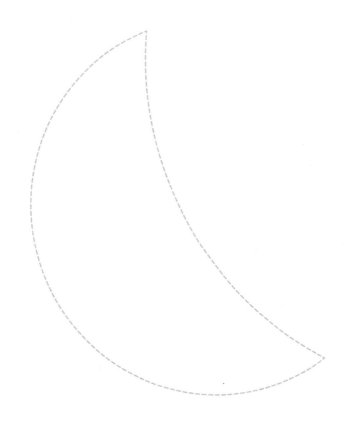

One evening, Harold decided to go on an adventure. "Let's go together!"

Join Harold for an adventure! Trace the moon to light the way.

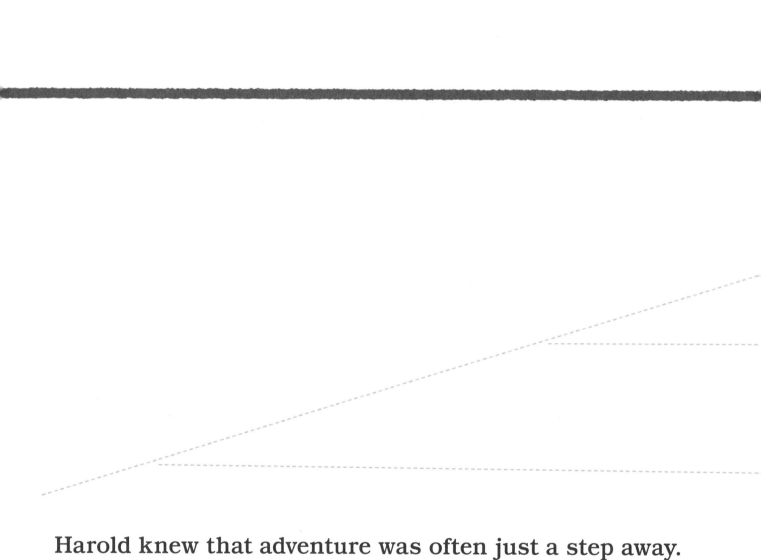

Harold knew that adventure was often just a step away.
But to take that first step, he needed a path to walk on.
"I'll draw this side. You draw that side!"

Help Harold complete the path. Draw some trees, buildings, animals,
and anything else you can imagine around the path.

And he needed a doorway to adventure.

So Harold drew a door.

Connect the dots.

11

Harold swung open the door, which gave a loud creak.
He saw a wide-open field. The field felt rather empty,
but Harold knew how to fix that.

"Come on! Let's fill the field with flowers!"

Color in Harold's flowers. Then add some more plants to the field.

It started to rain, which the flowers liked a lot.
But Harold wanted to stay dry.

Trace the umbrella to help Harold stay dry. Draw silly things that could be falling from the sky, like rubber balls, toys, cats, and dogs.

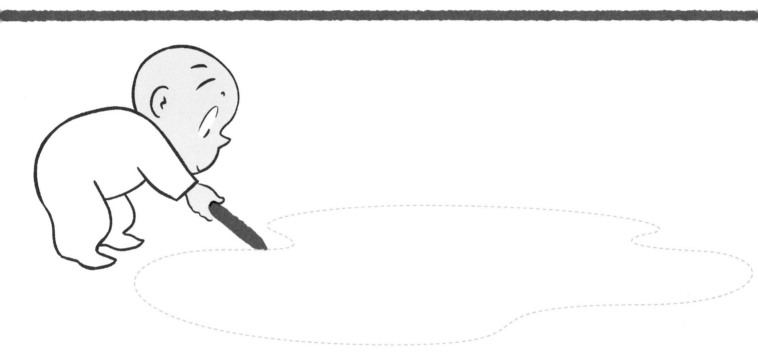

Suddenly, Harold heard something coming
from the ground. It sounded like water!
Luckily, Harold knew just what he had to do.
"Help me dig a hole!"

Trace the dotted line to help Harold draw a large hole in the ground.

You dug up some pretty cool things! Find and circle these things in the dirt:

☐ fossil ☐ shoe ☐ pine cone

☐ seashell ☐ toy truck

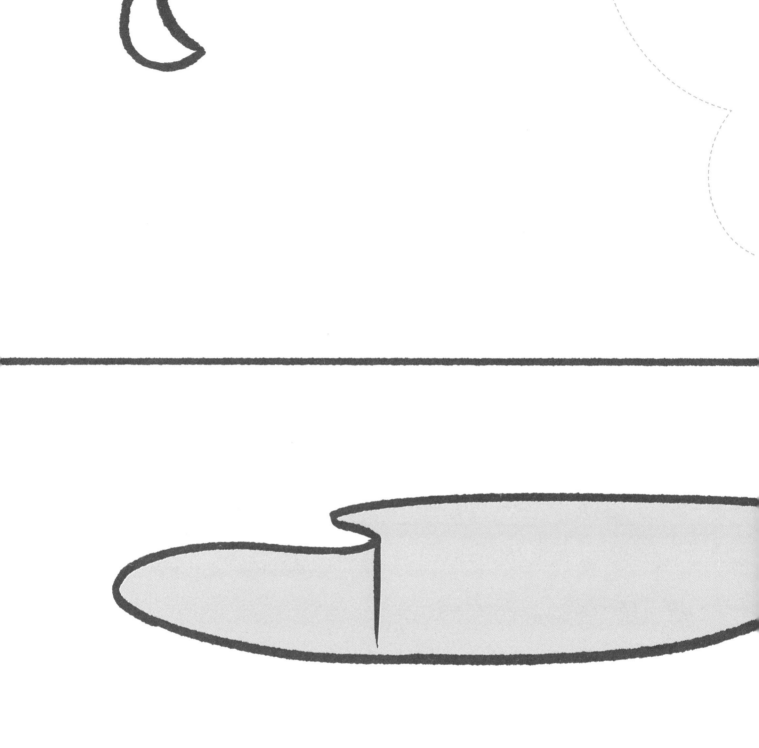

Harold looked down into the hole.

It seemed quite deep, so he came up with a plan.

"Let's tie a rope to a tree and climb into the hole!"

Help Harold finish drawing a tree. Then draw a rope around the tree and put the other end in the hole.

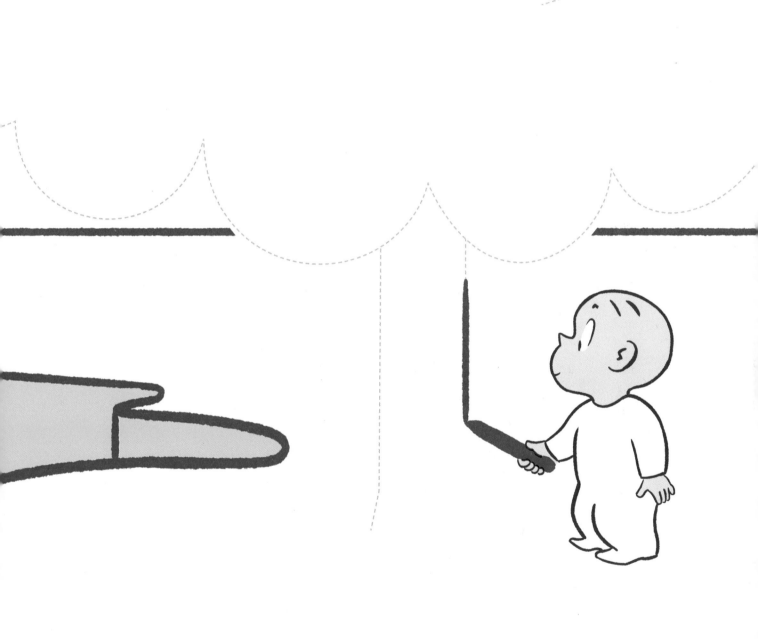

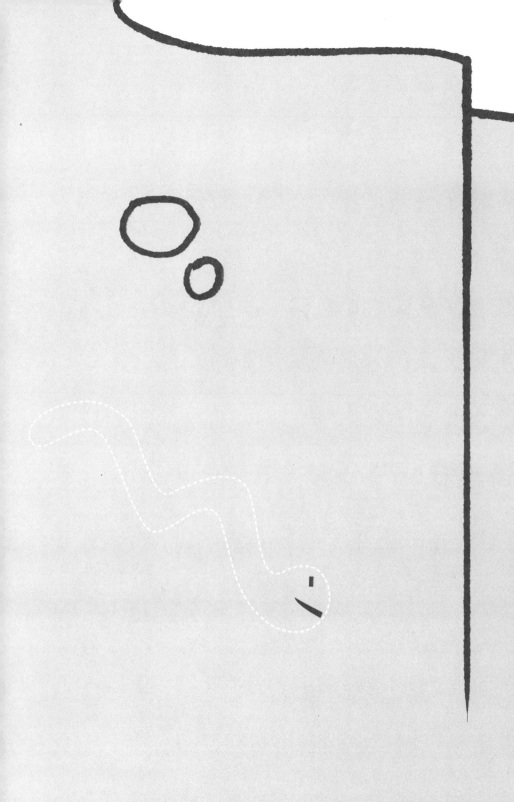

Down Harold went. Down, down, down.

Draw anything you think Harold may find in the sides of the hole—bugs, rocks, worms, or anything else you can imagine!

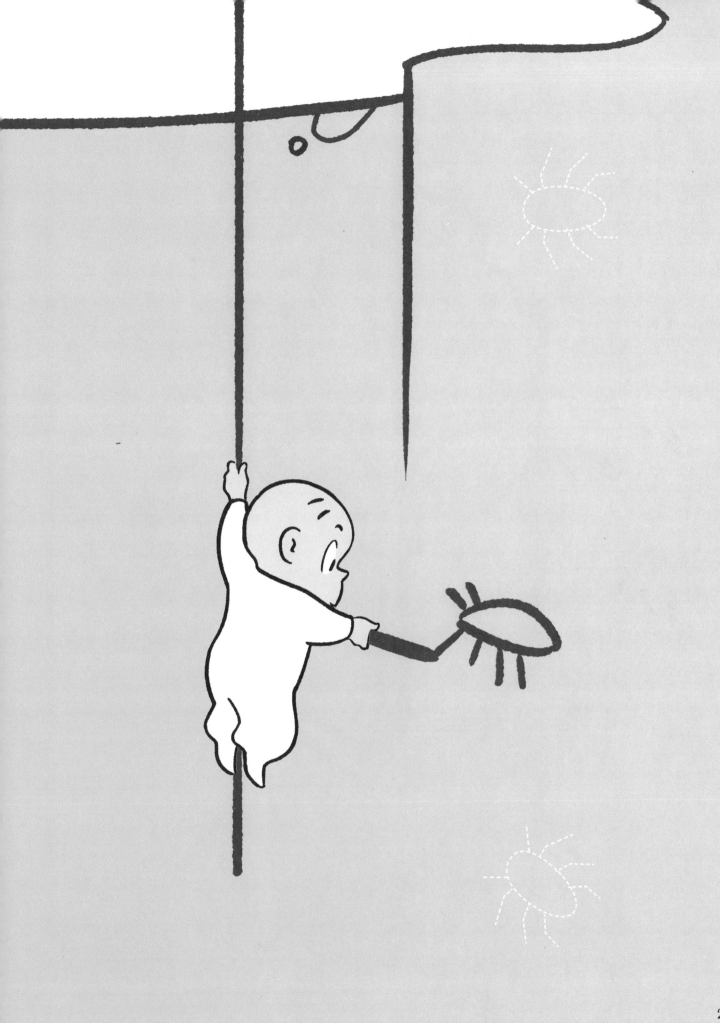

BEETLE 1

There are so many cool bugs! Spot the 5 differences between these two beetles and circle what's different on beetle 2.

BEETLE 2

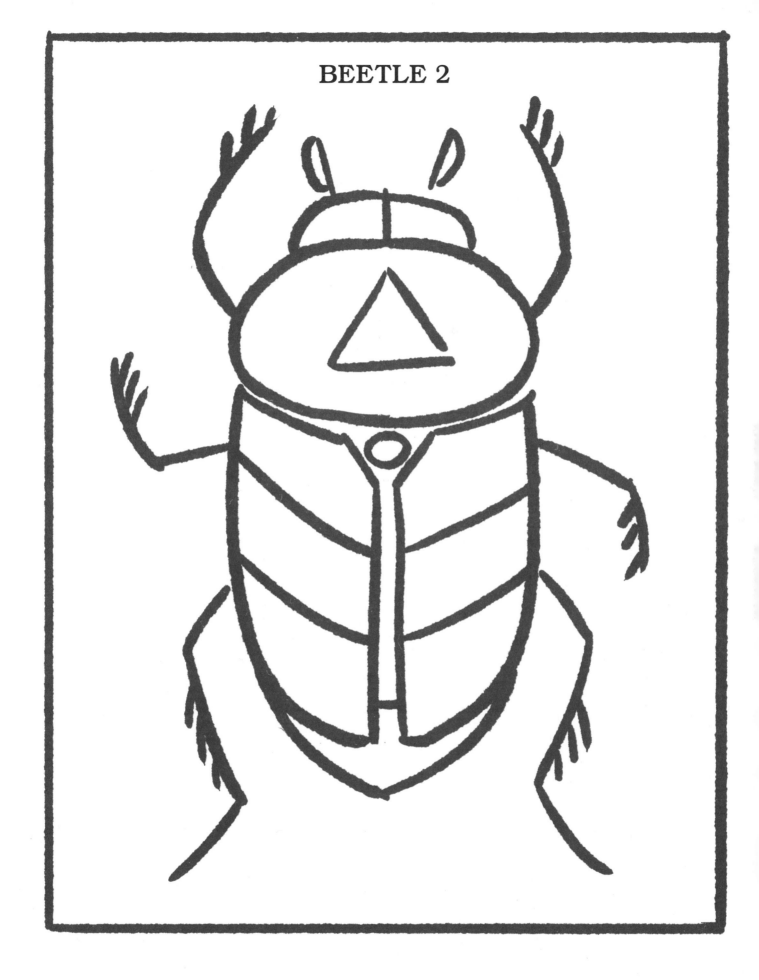

That was certainly an adventure!

Harold needed a place to land, so he drew one.

Trace the dashed lines to find out where Harold will land!
What else can you add to the scene? What would live down here? Draw it!

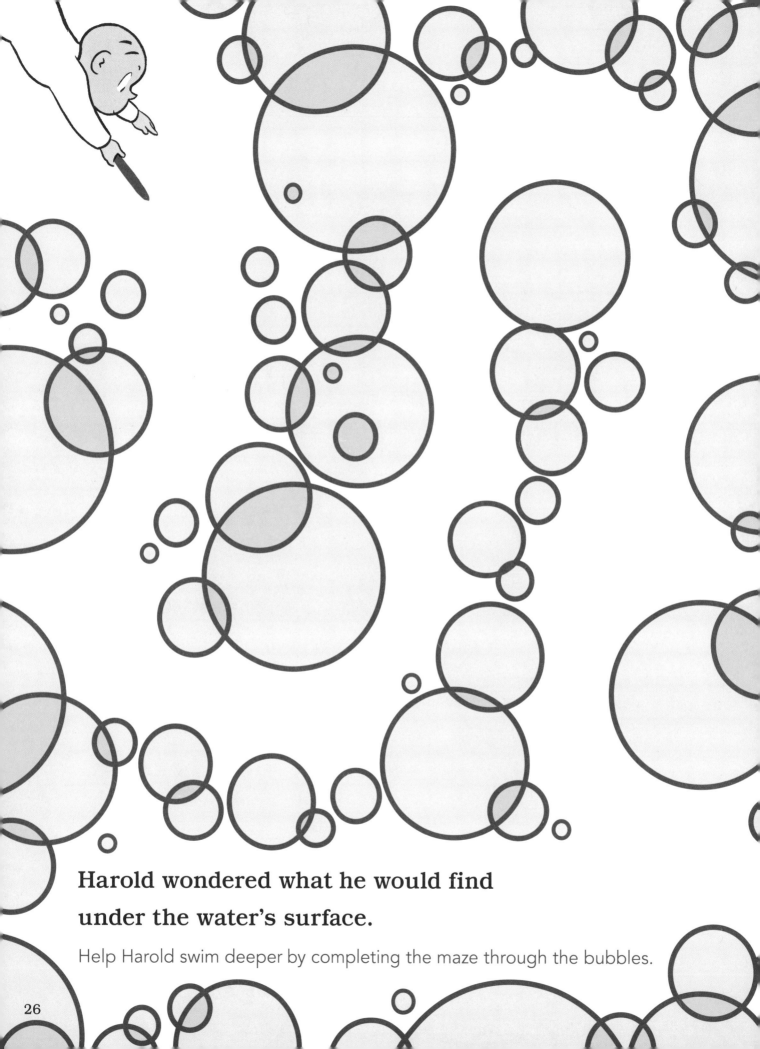

Harold wondered what he would find under the water's surface.

Help Harold swim deeper by completing the maze through the bubbles.

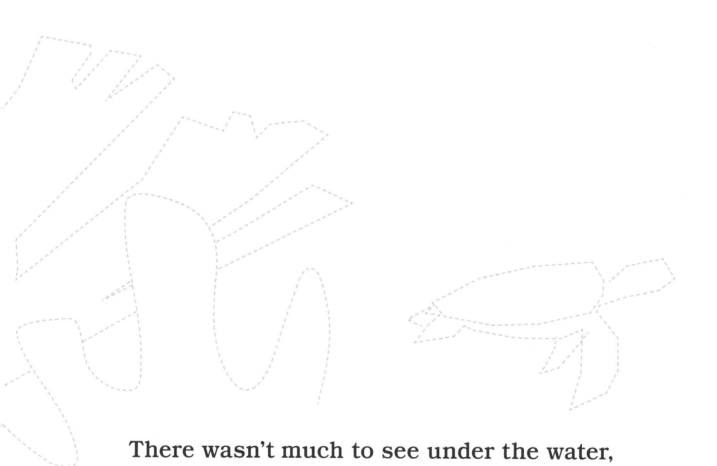

**There wasn't much to see under the water,
so Harold drew a coral reef to explore.
"Let's fill it with fish!"**

Help Harold fill in the coral reef with fun things to look at by tracing
the dashed lines and drawing anything else you can imagine!

Harold had always dreamed of swimming with the dolphins, and now seemed a fine time to make his dreams come true.

Trace the dashed lines to give Harold a pod of dolphins to swim with. Be sure to color them in!

Then Harold spotted something shiny underwater.

"Let's dive deeper! We'll need scuba gear."

Give Harold scuba gear by tracing the dashed lines. Then trace the dashed lines on the next page to discover all there is under the sea.

In no time, Harold came upon something quite remarkable.
"Look at that! Can you help me figure out what it is?"

Connect the dots to find out what Harold sees!

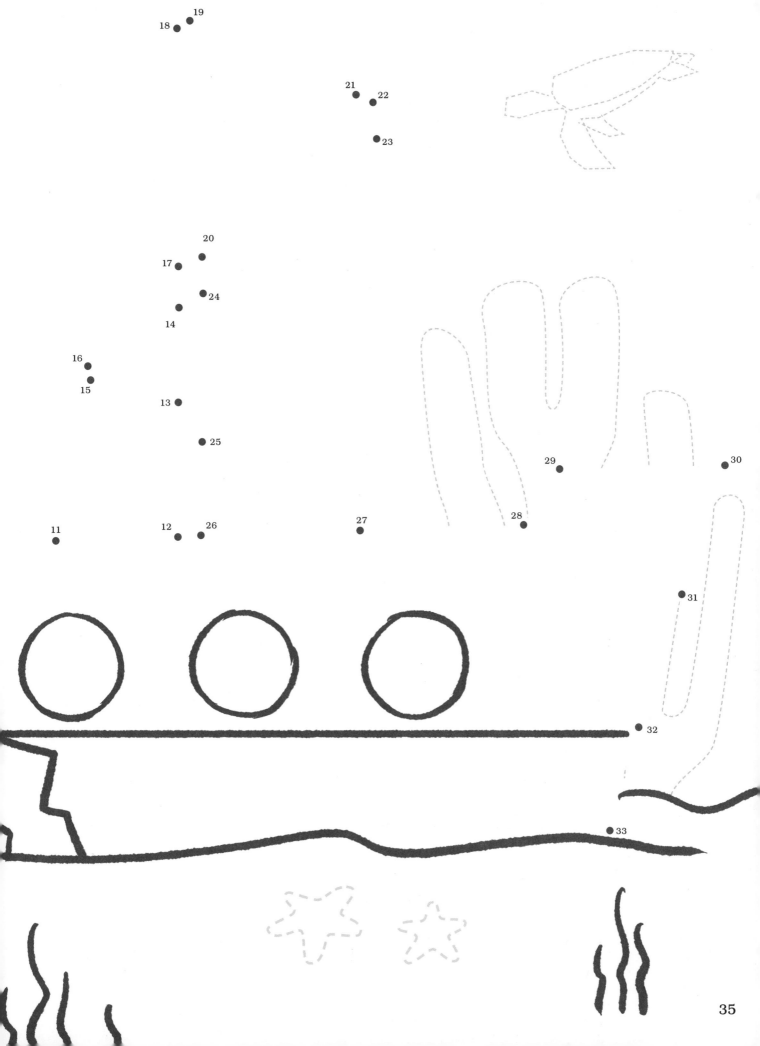

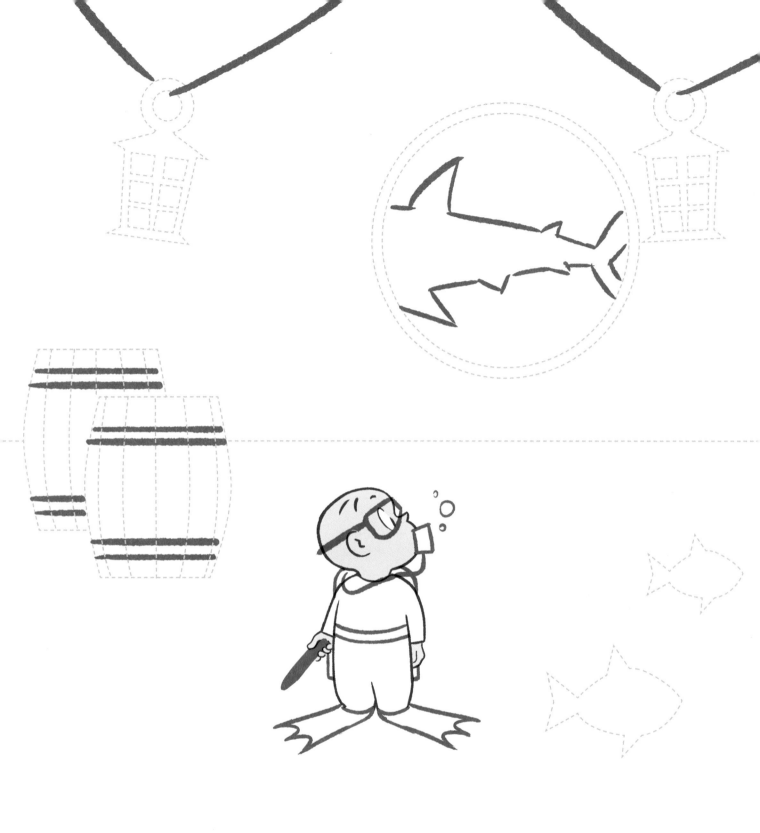

Harold explored inside the ship. He admired all the sunken treasures.

Trace the dashed lines and draw other sunken treasures on the ship's deck.

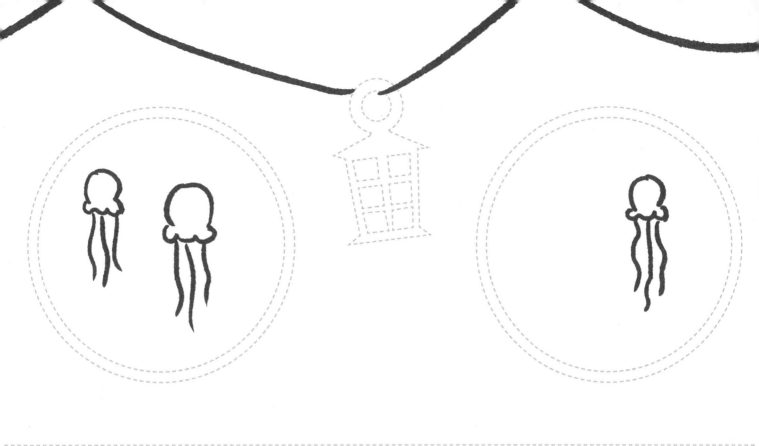

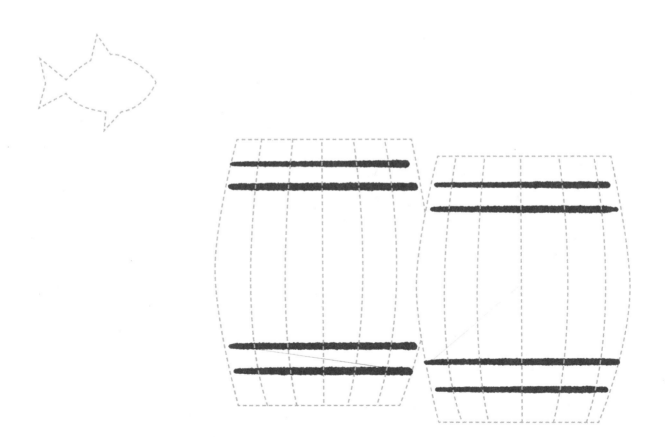

Suddenly, he saw something amazing.

"Look! Treasure chests! I wonder what's inside."

Trace the dashed lines to discover what's in the big chest.
Draw what you imagine is in the other chest, like jewels,
coins, and anything else you'd like to find inside.

38

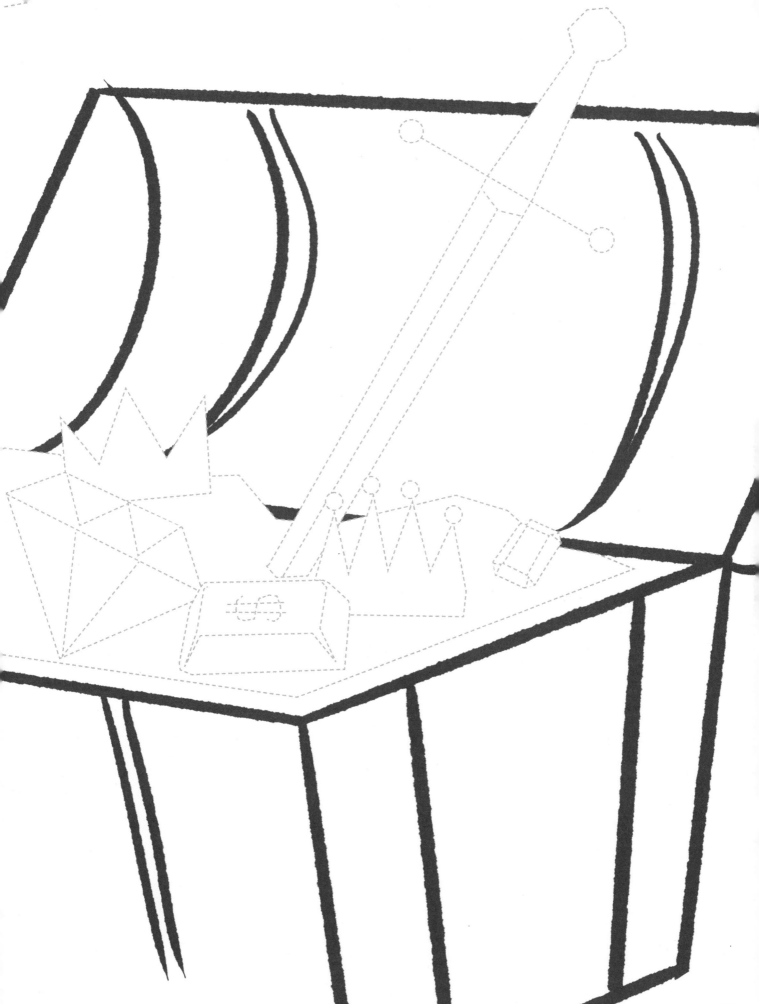

Harold reached for the treasure,
but a splashing noise distracted him.
"Monster!"

Connect the dots to complete the sea monster. Then give it some extra features like horns, spikes, and scales.

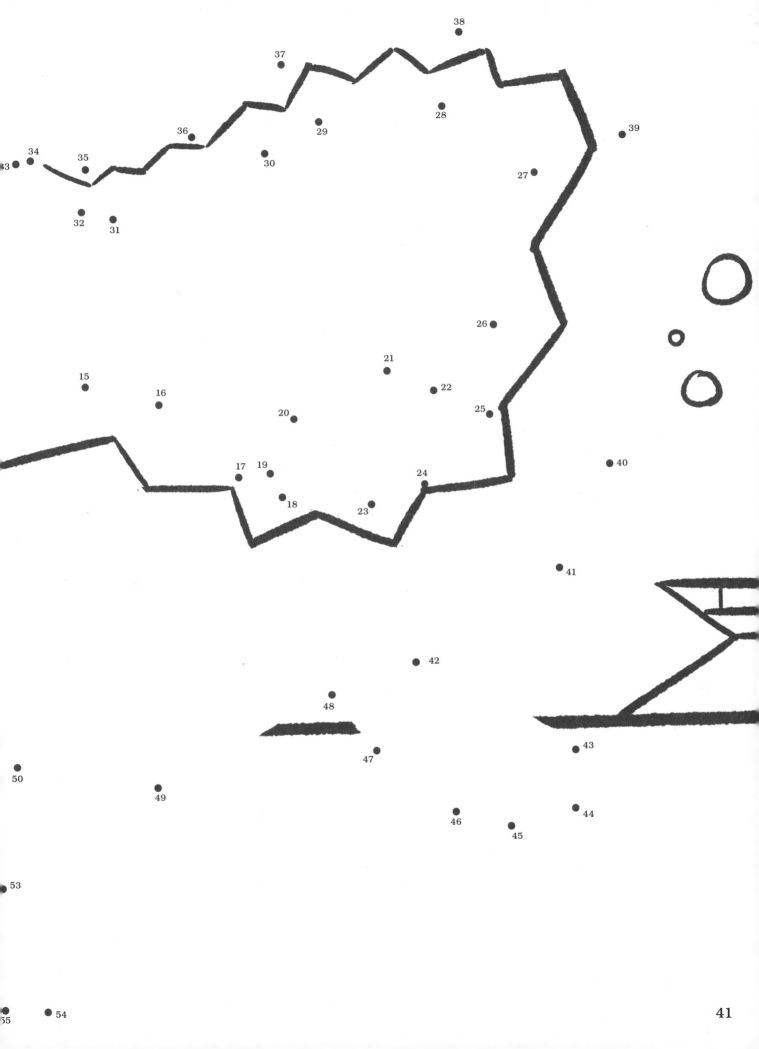

"Quick! We need a way out of here!"

Draw a way to get to the surface of the water. It could be
a giant fish or a long strand of seaweed! Use your imagination
to come up with something unique.

Harold broke through the water's surface,
but he was growing tired.
"We need a boat to rest on!"

Connect the dots to reveal the boat.

Harold climbed aboard the boat.
"Look! It's a pirate ship!"

Trace the dashed lines and color in the flag, adding any pirate-y details you'd like!

Harold knew the only way to survive among
pirates was to pretend to be one.
"Help! We need disguises!"

Trace the dashed lines to give Harold a disguise.
Be sure to color in the disguise!

But Harold was spotted even with his disguise.

Connect the dots and add some more pirates to the ship.

**Before Harold could get away, the pirates surrounded him.
They needed Harold's help.**

Help Harold choose the right path on the map to the island with the buried treasure.
X marks the spot!

Harold looked out at the water.

"There's nothing for miles. We need a spyglass!"

Trace the dashed lines to complete the scene. Decorate it any way you'd like.

Harold grabbed the spyglass and peered into the distance.

"Aha! I found it!"

Connect the dots to reveal the island Harold is looking at.

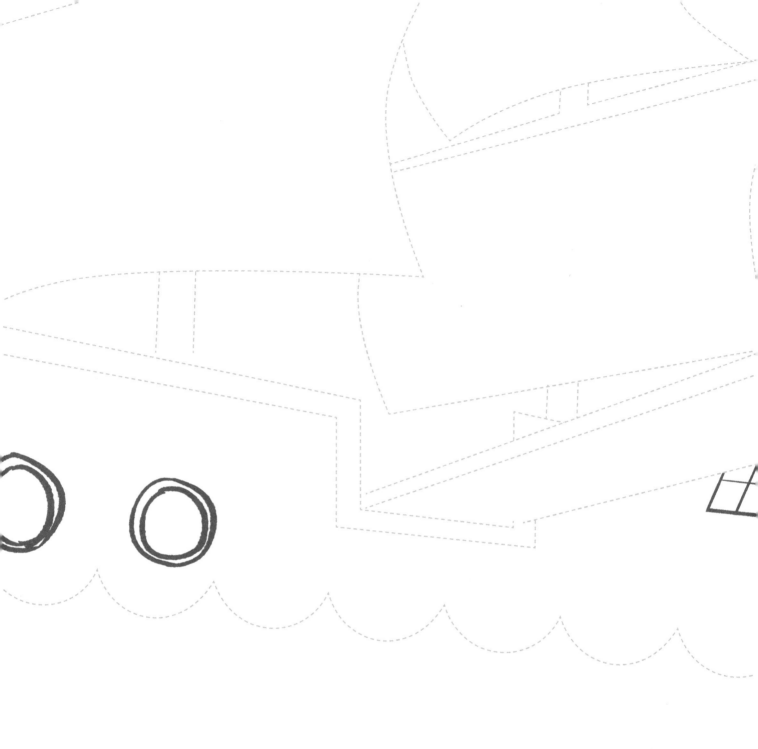

Finding buried treasure seemed like an excellent adventure.

So Harold decided to go visit the island next.

"Quick! We need a way off the boat!"

Trace the dashed lines to create a plank for Harold to walk.
Draw anything you think might be swimming in the water under the plank.

Find the two octopuses that are exactly the same.

Harold splashed into the water. And he made
a big wave to carry him away from the ship.

Trace the dashed lines to create a wave to push Harold closer to the island.
What else might be floating in the wave? Draw it!

But the island was too far away. So
Harold drew a surfboard.

Decorate Harold's surfboard.

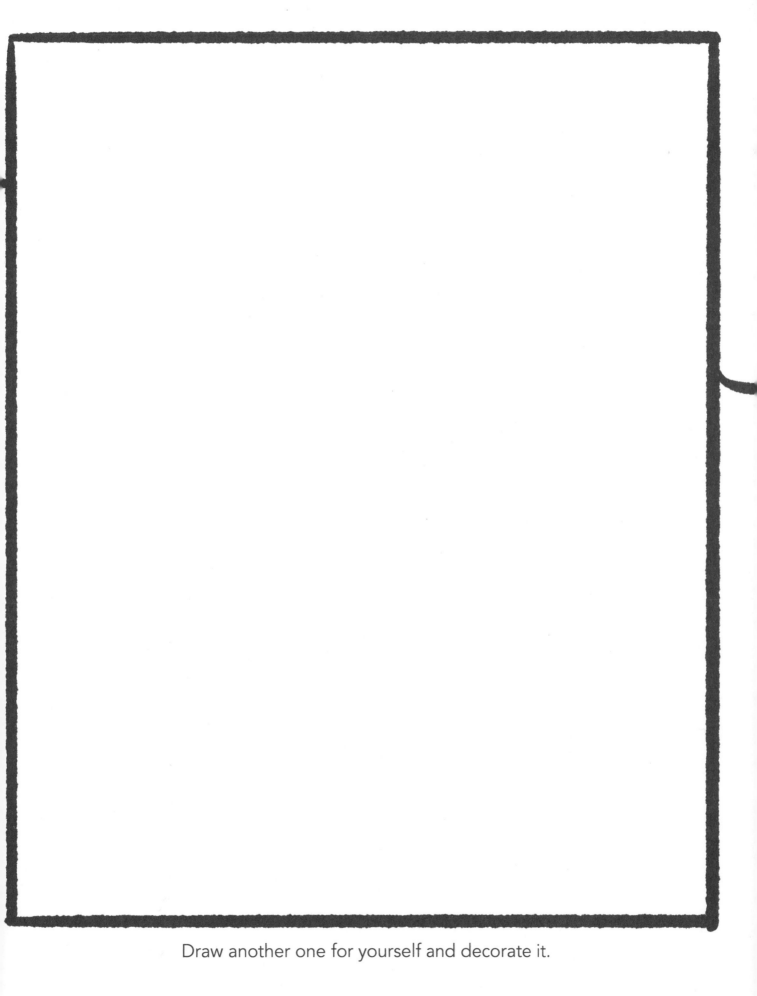

Draw another one for yourself and decorate it.

And he drew a friend to help him get to the island.

Connect the dots to find out who Harold's new friend is.

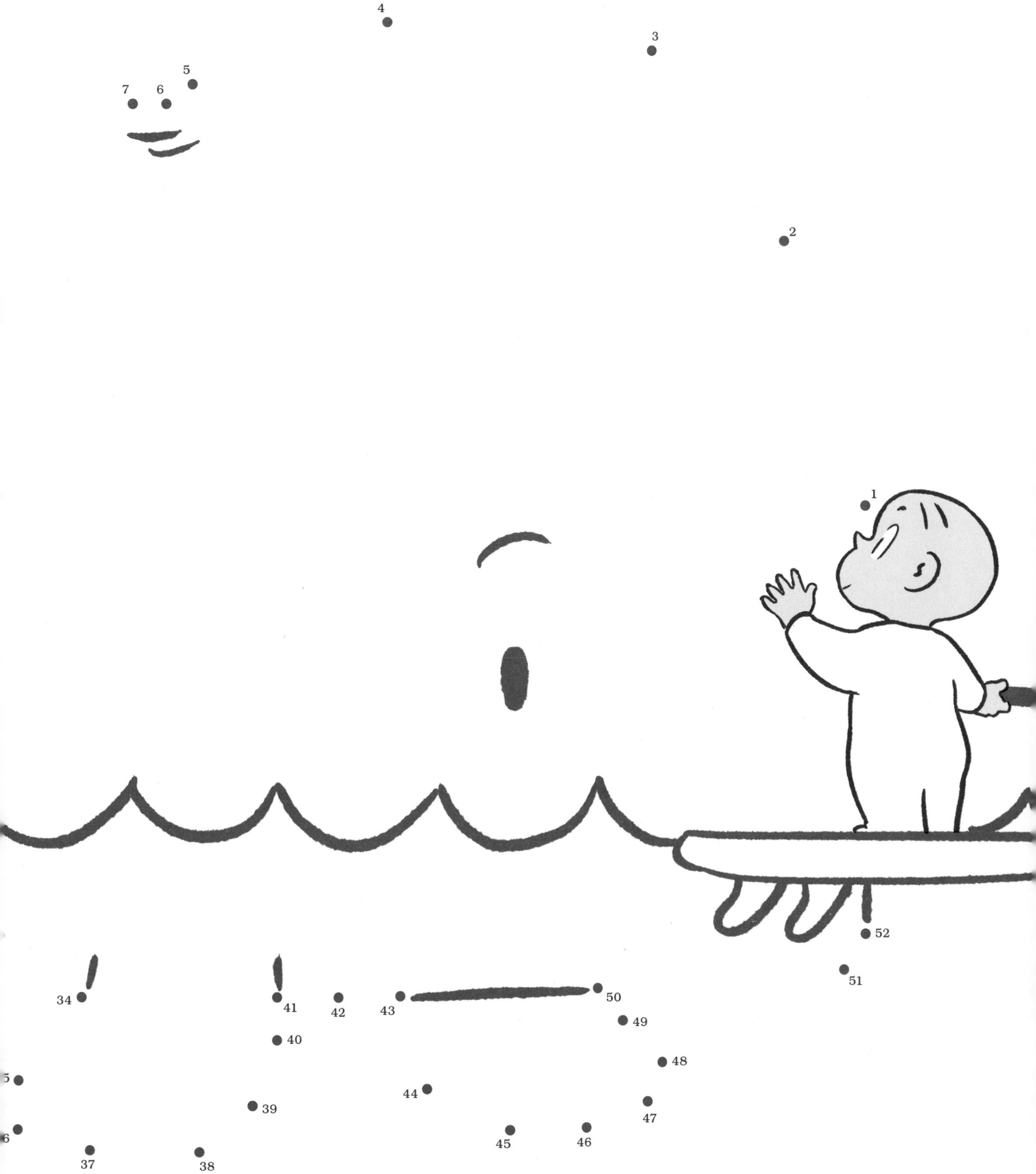
1
2
3
4
5
6
7
34
37
38
39
40
41
42
43
44
45
46
47
48
49
50
51
52

Unfortunately, Harold's whale-speak was a bit rusty.
"Can you help me figure out what he's saying?"

Decode the message to find out what the whale is saying.

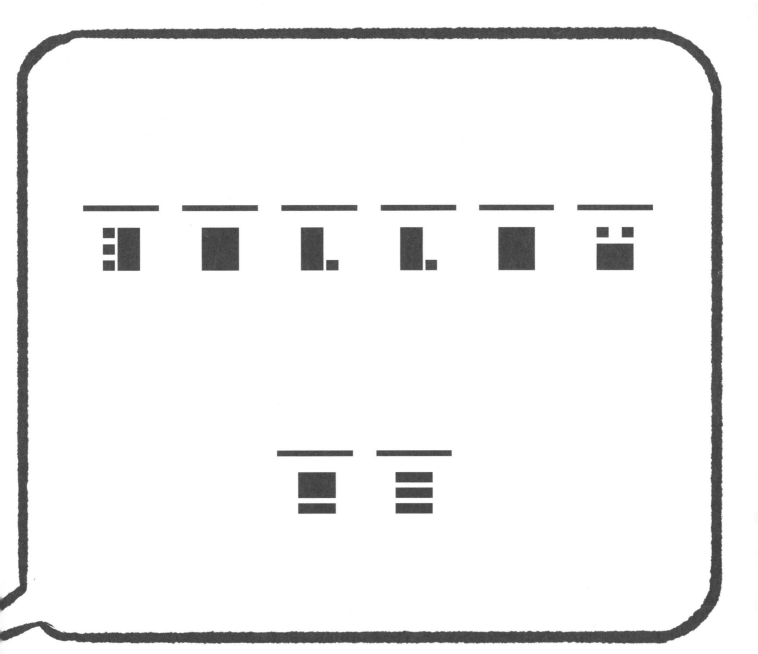

Key:

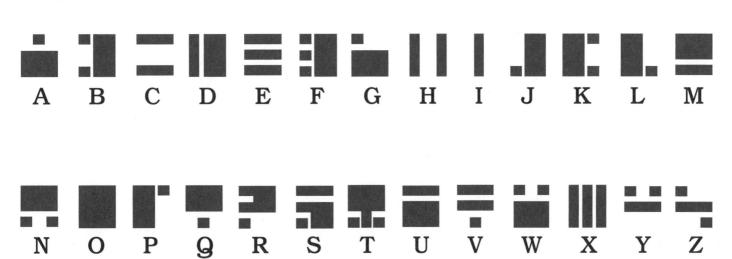

Harold followed the whale for some time.
Finally, he called, "Land, ho!"

Trace the dashed lines to reveal an island. Add anything
you can imagine living there.

Harold thanked the whale,

who replied with a giant spout of water.

Add a spout of water coming from the whale's head. It can be as big as you like! Might something else fly out of the whale's spout, like a fish or a toy or anything else you can imagine? Draw it!

The treasure map told Harold to dig near a patch of three trees.

"Can you help me find the way?"

Complete the maze by drawing a line along the path that leads to three trees.

Harold checked his map.

"We did it! Now we just need to dig up the treasure."

Trace the dashed lines to reveal where the treasure is.

What did you dig out of the hole this time? Draw it!

**Down Harold dug. Down, down, down.
Until he found something!**

Connect the dots to discover what Harold found.

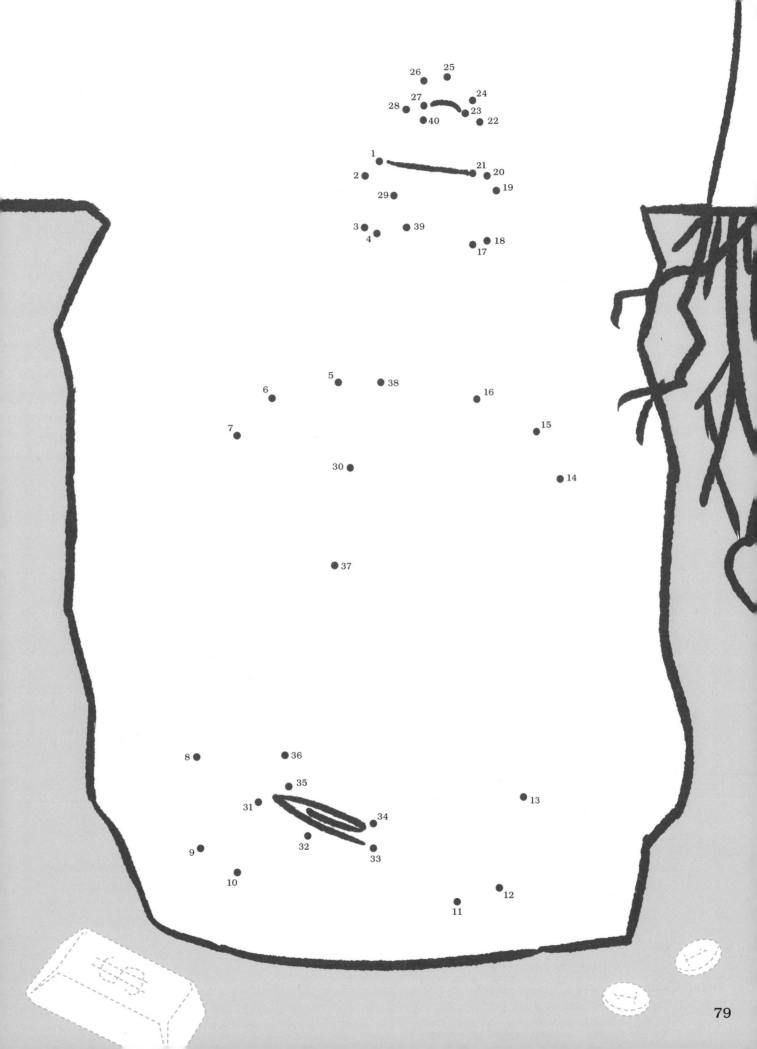

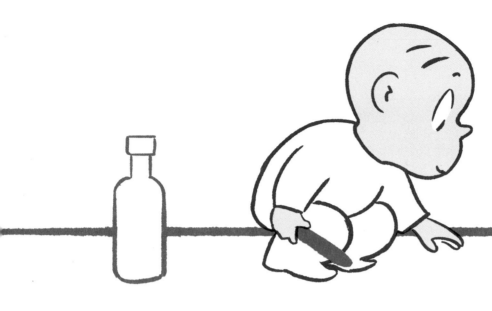

Key:

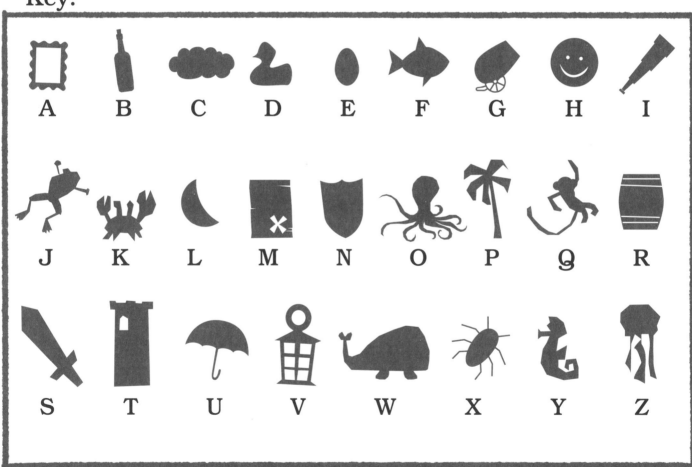

"Look! A clue fell out."

Help Harold decode the clue!

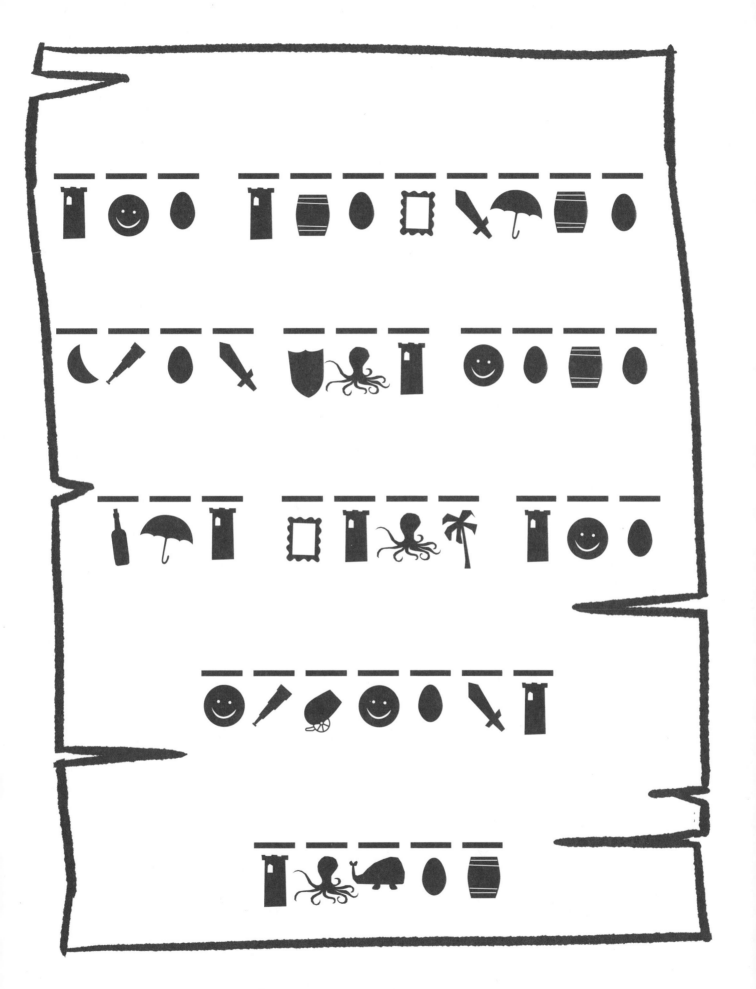

**Harold looked around, but he didn't see a tower.
"Can you help me get to the top of the tree?"**

Draw a way for Harold to climb the tree. You could add branches to climb on,
give him a ladder, build a slingshot. It's up to you! Use your imagination.

Harold squinted. In the distance, he could *almost* see a tower. "What should I use this time to see farther?"

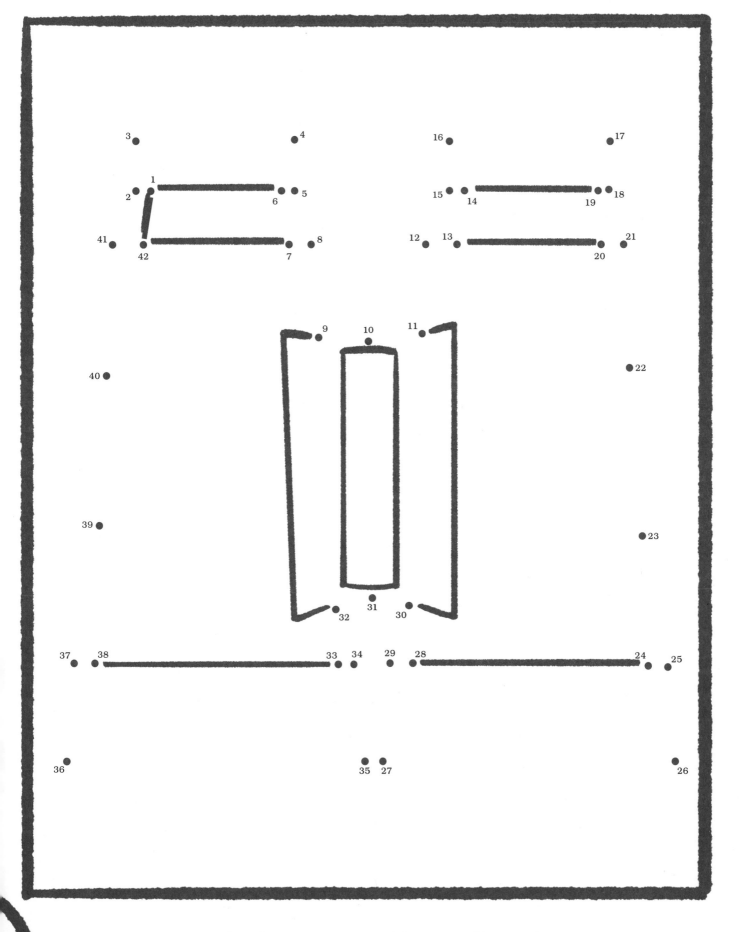

Connect the dots to give Harold a pair of binoculars!

"There! Do you see it?"

Draw anything you can imagine seeing far off in the distance.

"Not there. There!"

Harold pointed farther away.

Connect the dots to find out what Harold sees.

Harold looked toward the tower.

"It's too far to walk. We need to fly!"

Draw a way to fly to the tower with Harold. It could be
a hot-air balloon, a set of wings, or even an airplane.

Harold flew through the sky until suddenly the wind picked up and Harold started to fall. "Help!"

Draw a way to get to the ground safely—a parachute, a trampoline, a slide, anything you can imagine!

Harold's feet hit the ground, but the ground was not ground at all. It was hot lava!

Trace Harold's rocks to make a safe path across the lava.

The lava quickly covered the rocks Harold used to get across. "Quick! Find another way across!"

Choose the right path to get to the other side with Harold.

"I'll keep going. You catch up!"

Complete the maze to find your way through the trees for Harold so you can find the treasure together.

SCENE 1

There are 8 differences between these two scenes.
Circle what's different on scene 2.

SCENE 2

Harold left you the things you'll need in order to catch up to him. Find these objects and circle them:

☐ compass ☐ spyglass ☐ boots ☐ beach ball ☐ water bottle

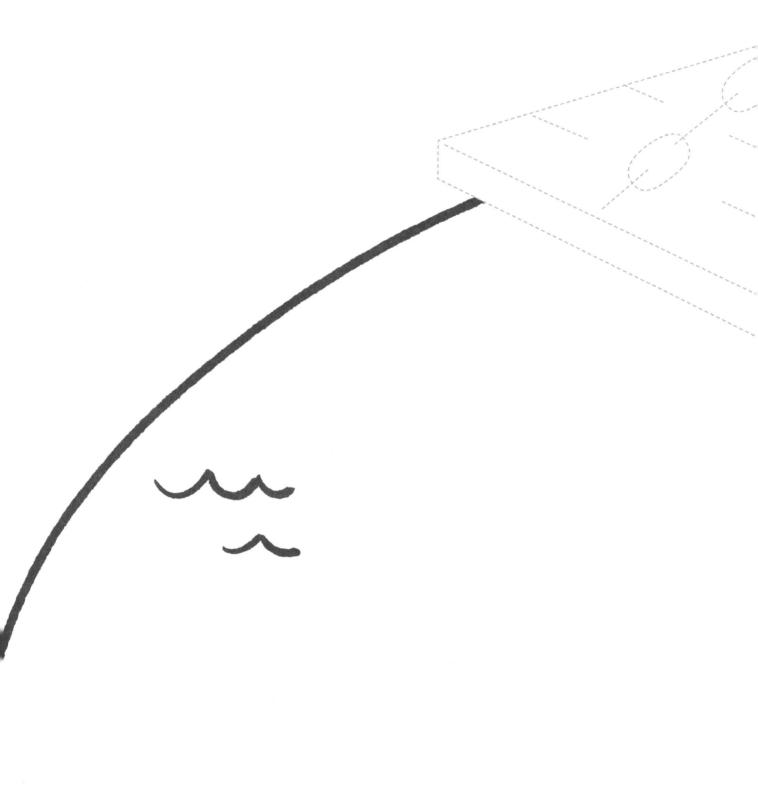

It's a moat! Connect the dashed lines to reveal a drawbridge so you can get to the other side. Is there anything living in the moat? Draw it!

Harold waited by the tower! Up above, he heard the flapping of wings. "Dragon!"

Draw flames coming from the dragon's mouth.

To face a dragon, Harold knew, one must be a knight! So he drew himself a suit of armor.

Trace the dashed lines to reveal Harold's suit of armor.
Decorate it any way you'd like!

The door was locked and the tower
was quite a bit taller than Harold had expected.
Luckily, he was an excellent climber!

Complete the maze to find a way up the blocks.

At the tower's highest window,
there were no more footholds to climb.
"Can you help me get to the roof?"

Draw a way to get Harold to the tower's roof. It could be a trampoline, a slingshot, a grappling hook, or anything else. Use your imagination!

At the top of the tower, Harold saw a giant treasure chest.

He had found the pirate's treasure.

But to get it, he would have to get past the dragon.

Connect the dots to reveal the treasure chest.

Harold approached the dragon. It was not as large as it had looked from the ground, and Harold wondered if it might be hungry.

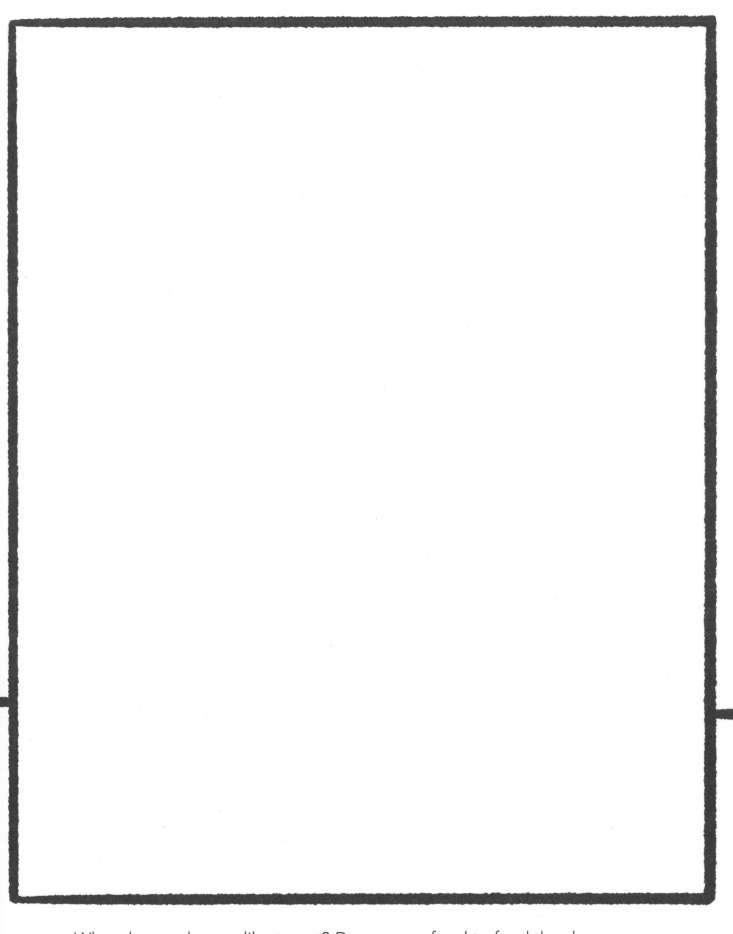

What does a dragon like to eat? Draw some food to feed the dragon.

When the dragon didn't move, Harold realized something.
Perhaps the dragon was not hungry at all. Perhaps it was
tired. So Harold drew a bed for it.

Trace the dashed lines to complete the bed around the dragon.

As Harold's eyes closed, he thought that he had had quite enough adventure for one day.

Trace the dashed lines.

HOW TO DRAW HAROLD

Follow the arrows in each step.

STEP 1

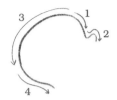

STEP 2

STEP 3

STEP 4

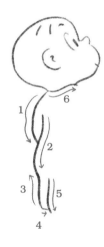

STEP 5

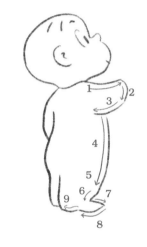

STEP 6

Now try drawing Harold on your own!

Draw pictures of you and Harold together from your adventure!

Answers to puzzles:

pages 16-17

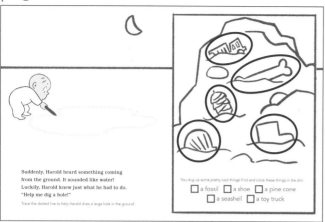

pages 22-23

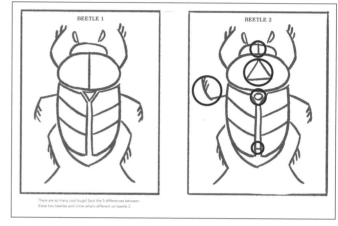

pages 26-27

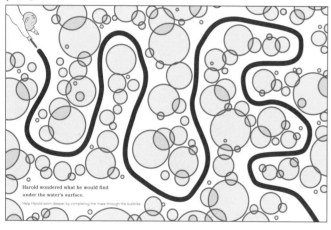

pages 52-53

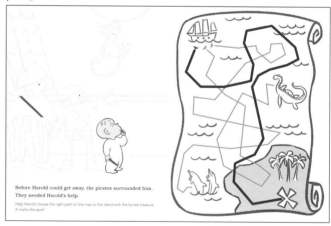

pages 60-61

pages 68-69

pages 74-75

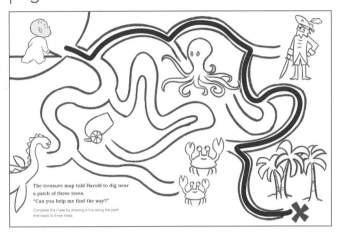

pages 80-81

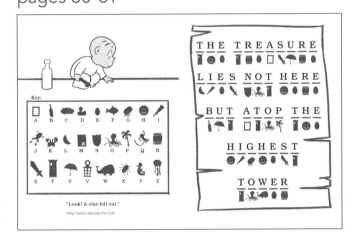

pages 96-97

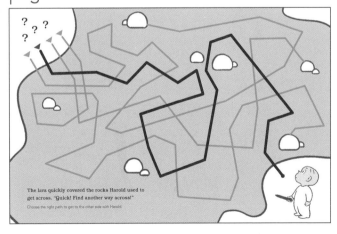

pages 98-99

pages 100-101

pages 102-103

pages 110-111

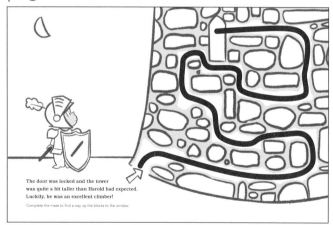